Bugs in My Hair?!

Catherine Stier

illustrated by

Tammie Lyon

Albert Whitman & Company, Chicago, Illinois

To anyone who has ever
cried out with dismay, "Bugs in my hair?!"
with sympathetic understanding from
someone who's been there.—C.S.

For Irelyn Marie Lyon—
I love you.—T.L.

Library of Congress Cataloging-in-Publication Data

Stier, Catherine.
Bugs in my hair?! / written by Catherine Stier ; illustrated by Tammie Lyon.
p. cm.
Summary: When immaculately groomed Ellie gets head lice she is terribly upset,
but once she learns some facts about the creatures, she calms down
and figures out a way to help her classmates.
ISBN 978-0-8075-0908-1 (hardcover)
ISBN 978-0-8075-0909-8 (paperback)
[1. Lice—Fiction. 2. Schools—Fiction.] I. Lyon, Tammie, ill. II. Title.
PZ7.S8556295Bu 2008 [E]—dc22 2007024250

The design is by Carol Gildar.

For more information about Albert Whitman & Company,
please visit our web site at www.albertwhitman.com.

Note to
Concerned Grownups

It's no fun to discover bugs in your child's hair. But what should you do (after reassuring your child and calming down yourself)?

Most doctors, departments of public health, and schools advise first using an FDA-approved, over-the-counter lice treatment containing pyrethrins or permethrin. Several prominent child health organizations maintain that the removal of nits (lice eggs and their shell casings) after such a treatment is not necessary, but a personal choice.

However, some children are sensitive to lice treatment products, and strains of lice have developed resistance to some of these products. Therefore, other experts advocate using a specially designed comb to remove lice and nits, over a period of days or weeks, as a first approach when it is practical.

Parents should first consult their pediatrician for recommendations on the best treatment option for their child.

Parents and children alike should know that head lice do not cause serious harm or transmit any diseases. "Getting lice" does not reflect on the cleanliness of the child or home. It truly is an occurrence that can be shrugged off with the understanding that sometimes "these things happen."

Catherine Stier

E llie LaFleur did things just so. Each evening, Ellie filed her nails to perfect ovals. She chose a snazzy outfit to wear the next day. And Ellie always washed her long, lovely locks with Princess Luxury Shampoo.

At school, when Alex spilled milk on his football jersey, he shrugged.

"These things happen," he said.

"Not to me," sniffed Ellie.

And when Morgan's braid unraveled, she shrugged.

"These things happen," said Morgan.

"Not to me," sniffed Ellie.

And it was true. Those kinds of things *never* happened to Absolutely Perfect Ellie.

But one Friday morning, something did happen to Ellie.

Her head began to itch. And itch. AND ITCH. When Ellie couldn't stand it any longer, she raised her hand.

"Ms. Snick, may I go to the nurse's office? I've been scratching and scratching. Someone at the shampoo factory must have messed up the formula for my Princess Luxury Shampoo! And now my delicate skin is very itchy!"

Ms. Snick's eyebrows popped up. "Yes, Ellie, if your head is itchy you may certainly go to the nurse's office."

So Ellie stood, smoothed her darling raspberry skirt, and sashayed out the door, scratching all the way.

When Ellie arrived at the office, the nurse whisked her in.

"We've had two other students with itchy heads this week," said the nurse.

Aha! Someone else must use Princess Luxury Shampoo! thought Ellie.

The nurse sat Ellie down and put on plastic gloves. She picked up strands of Ellie's hair and looked at her scalp. Then she turned to the phone and called Ellie's mom.

Whoa, thought Ellie. It must be serious!

Mom arrived at the nurse's office looking worried. She and the nurse peered down at Ellie's hair. "See?" said the nurse.

"Oh, no!" said Mom. "It's a . . . *bug!*"

Ellie's eyes grew wide. Her lip quivered, her body shivered, and before she could stop herself, Ellie blurted out: "BUGS IN MY HAIR?! WHAT DO YOU MEAN?"

"Don't worry, Ellie," said the nurse. "They're called head lice. And we know how to get rid of them."

Ellie's tummy flipped. *"Lice?"* she whispered. "How could *I* have lice?"

The nurse handed papers to Ellie's mom.
Scary papers, all about scary lice, thought Ellie.
"I think I'd like to go home," she said.
"Don't feel bad, Ellie," Mom said on the
quiet ride back. "These things happen."
"Not to *me*," sniffed Ellie.

At home, Ellie sat on her hands. She tried not to scratch. She tried not to cry. Mostly, she tried *not* to think about the horrid things hanging out in her hair.

Ellie's mom read the scary papers and called the doctor.

"Well, Ellie," said Mom. "We'll buy a special get-rid-of-lice treatment to use on your hair. No Princess Luxury Shampoo this time! Then, I know you'll feel better if we comb out your hair to get the eggs, or nits, the lice have left behind."

"Gross," said Ellie glumly.

"And we'll wash your bedding and the clothes you've worn recently. We'll vacuum the floors and furniture," said Mom. "That should be the end of the lice."

So Ellie helped gather the bedding.

She helped put things that couldn't be washed in an airtight bag.
"Bye for a while, Susan," she told her doll.

Dad came home with the special get-rid-of-lice treatment.
Then Mom began to work the treatment through Ellie's hair.
Ellie sat wrapped in a towel, waiting, while the treatment
did its work.

Then Ellie had to sit even longer as Mom and Dad combed out the nits. Ellie sighed as the comb tugged through her hair over and over again.

As Ellie sat and sat, she daydreamed. She imagined herself
a pampered princess with her tresses tended by the royal hairdresser.

But even pretend princesses get bored. And curious. Ellie grew so
curious that she picked up the nurse's scary papers. *Disgusting*, she
thought as she read . . . but kind of interesting.

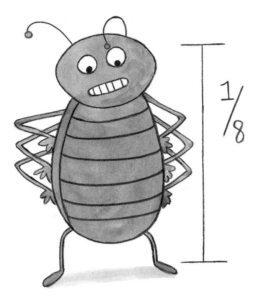

Later Ellie told her father, "Go ahead. Ask me anything about lice!"

"Okay," said Dad. "How big are lice?"

"A louse—" said Ellie, "that's the word for just one bug—is about one-eighth of an inch long. Tiny, but big enough to see with your eyes."

"What do they eat?" asked Dad.

Ellie made a face. "Human blood! They bite into the skin on your head and suck the blood out."

"Yuk!" said Dad. "Last question. How does a person get lice in the first place?"

"They can crawl," said Ellie, wiggling her fingers. "If you lean your head close to someone else's, they might crawl over. They could even crawl onto a hat or comb—though they can't live long away from your hair. But that's why you shouldn't share things that touch your hair."

Dad looked impressed. "How do you know so much?" he asked.

"I read those scary papers from the nurse. Only, they're not so scary. They just have facts about lice," said Ellie. "I wish that when I first found out I had lice, I had known." Then Ellie stopped. She had an idea. An *incredible* idea. Something she could do all by herself.

"You know," Mom said just then. "I've read those scary papers so much, I have a name for them, too. I call them 'Everything You Never Wanted to Know about Lice.'"

"I've got one!" Ellie said, cracking up. She could barely get the words out. "Little LOUSE on the HAIRY!"

Ellie howled so hard she fell over.

On Monday Ellie got ready to return to school. She put on her snazziest outfit and clipped sparkly barrettes into her hair. Then she tucked her amazing idea, the thing she had worked on that weekend, inside her backpack. She and her mom headed to school—and straight to the nurse's office.

"I'm bug-free now," said Ellie. "Take a look!"

The nurse checked Ellie's hair. "All's clear!" she declared.

Ellie took a deep breath. "Ta-da!" she said. And Ellie brought out her amazing idea. The nurse took it and looked it over.

"Ellie," said the nurse. "This is terrific! May I make copies? When I give parents information about lice, I'd like to give this to the kids. Your letter will help them know they're not alone."

"That's just what I had in mind!" Ellie said proudly.

This is what Ellie's letter said:

Dear kid who just found out you have

lice

DON'T PANIC!

I know the idea that you have **bugs** in your hair is freaking you out. I freaked out when I found I had **lice**, too. (Here's a drawing of me when I got the news.)

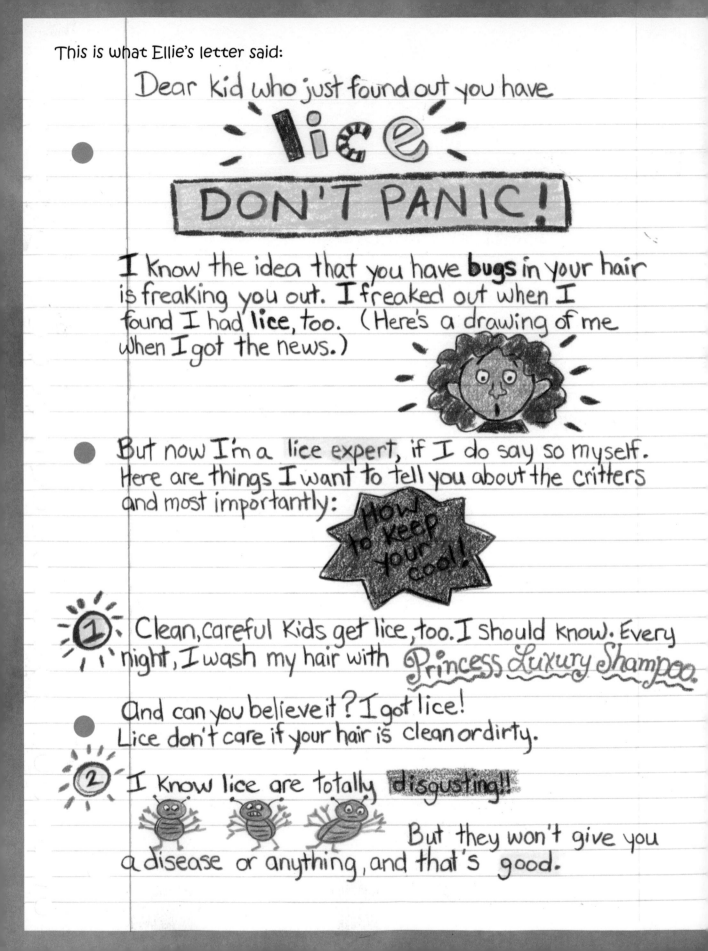

But now I'm a lice expert, if I do say so myself. Here are things I want to tell you about the critters and most importantly:

How to keep your cool!

①. Clean, careful kids get lice, too. I should know. Every night, I wash my hair with *Princess Luxury Shampoo.*

And can you believe it? I got lice! Lice don't care if your hair is clean or dirty.

② I know lice are totally disgusting!!

But they won't give you a disease or anything, and that's good.

③ You **CAN** get rid of lice The school nurse probably gave you a stack of scary-looking papers.

DON'T WORRY The papers tell your parents all the important things to do. Like how you might use a special get-rid-of-lice treatment — **NO** Princess Luxury Shampoo this time! And how to comb out all the eggs. (ugh!).

Here's my advice — **RELAX** and try to make the best of it. Like, when my parents combed my hair, I pretended I was getting ready for a fancy ball. And if you read about lice, you'll find they are interesting-in a gross-out kind of way.

So don't be **sad** or feel scared or bad. This is just the kind of not-so-great stuff every kid has to deal with sometimes. You know, like spilling milk on your football jersey or losing a hair ribbon. (**Well,** maybe it is worse than that.)

BUT take it from me — sometimes these things happen! And you're going to be okay—REALLY!

Signed,

A third grader who has been there!

"Wow, Ellie," said the nurse and Mom together.

"Just hope it helps," said Ellie.

Then Ellie stood and waved goodbye. She smoothed her darling tangerine skirt and sashayed to her classroom. And this time, Ellie didn't scratch. Not one bit.